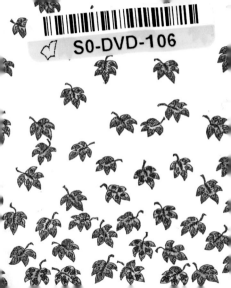

Alice in Wonderland

by Lewis Carroll
Retold by David Blair
Illustrated by Graham Evernden

Running Press
Philadelphia • Pennsylvania

A Running Press Miniature Edition™

Copyright © 1993 by Running Press.

Illustrations © 1993 by Graham Evernden. Printed in Singapore. All rights reserved under the Pan-American and International Copyright Conventions.

This book may be not reproduced in whole or in part in any form or by any means, electronic or mechanical, including photocopying, recording, or by any information storage and retrieval system now known or hereafter invented, without written permission from the publisher. The proprietary trade dress, including the size and format of this Running Press Miniature Edition™, is the property of Running Press. It may not be used or reproduced without the express written permission of Running Press.

Canadian representatives: General Publishing Co., Ltd., 30 Lesmill Road, Don Mills, Ontario M3B 2T6.

International representatives: Worldwide Media Services, Inc., 30 Montgomery Street, Jersey City, New Jersey 07302.

Library of Congress Cataloging-in-Publication Number 92-50804

ISBN 1-56138-246-9

This book may be ordered by mail from the publisher. Please include $1.00 for postage and handling.

But try your bookstore first!

Running Press Book Publishers
125 South Twenty-second Street
Philadelphia, Pennsylvania 19103

Chapter One

Down the Rabbit Hole

Alice was beginning to get very
tired of sitting by her sister on the
bank, and of having nothing to do.
She was considering whether
the pleasure of making a daisy chain
would be worth the trouble of

getting up and picking the daisies,
when suddenly a white rabbit with
pink eyes ran close by her.

There was nothing so *very* re-
markable in that; nor did Alice
think it *very* strange to hear the
Rabbit say to itself, "Oh dear! Oh
dear! I shall be too late!" When
the Rabbit actually *took a watch
out of its waistcoat pocket,* and
looked at it, and then hurried on,
Alice started to her feet. It flashed

across her mind that she had never before seen a rabbit with either a waistcoat pocket, or a watch to take out of it. Burning with curiosity, she ran across the field just in time to see the Rabbit pop down a large rabbit hole under the hedge.

In another moment down went Alice after it, never once considering how in the world she was to get out again.

The rabbit hole went straight

on like a tunnel for some way, and then dipped down so suddenly that Alice had not a moment to think about stopping herself from falling down what seemed to be a very deep well.

"Well!" thought Alice as she fell, "after this, I shall think nothing of tumbling down stairs!"

Down, down, down. Would the fall never come to an end? "I wonder how many miles I've fallen?" she said aloud. "I wonder if I shall fall right through the earth!"

Down, down, down. There was nothing else to do, so Alice soon began talking again. "Dinah'll miss me very much tonight, I should think!" (Dinah was the cat.) "I hope they remember her saucer of milk at teatime. Dinah, my dear! I wish you were down here with me!"

She felt that she was dozing

off, and had just begun to dream that she was walking with Dinah, when suddenly, *thump! thump!* down she came upon a heap of sticks and dry leaves.

Alice was not a bit hurt. Before her was another long passage, and the White Rabbit was still in sight, hurrying down it. Away went Alice like the wind, just in time to hear the Rabbit say, as it turned a corner, "Oh my ears and whiskers, how late it's getting!"

When Alice turned the corner, the Rabbit was no longer to be seen. Alice found herself in a long, low hall, which was lit by a row of lamps hanging from the roof.

There were doors all round the hall, but they were all locked. Sadly, Alice wondered how she was ever going to get out again.

Suddenly she came upon a little

glass table. There was nothing on it but a tiny golden key. Alice's first idea was that it might belong to one of the doors of the hall; but, alas! either the locks were too large, or the key was too small. Then she came upon a little door she had not noticed before. It was about fifteen inches high. She tried the key in the lock, and to her great delight, it fitted!

Beyond the door was the

loveliest garden you ever saw. How Alice longed to wander among those beds of bright flowers and cool fountains, but she could not even fit her head through the tiny doorway. "Oh, how I wish I could shut up like a telescope!" she thought.

There seemed to be no use in waiting by the little door, so Alice went back to the table. This time she found a little bottle on it. Tied around the neck of the bottle was a paper label with the words "DRINK ME" beautifully printed in large letters.

Wise little Alice was not going to do that in a hurry. "No, I'll look first," she said, "and see whether it's marked 'poison.'" However, this little bottle was not marked "poison," so Alice ventured to taste it. It tasted very nice (a sort of mixed flavor of cherrytart, custard, pineapple, roast turkey, toffy, and hot buttered toast), so Alice very soon finished it off.

"What a curious feeling!" said Alice, "I must be shutting up like a telescope!"

And so it was indeed: she was now only ten inches high—just the right size for going through the little door into that lovely garden!

But, alas! when she got to the door, she found she had forgotten the golden key. When she went back to the table for it, she was too small to reach it. Poor Alice sat down and cried.

Soon her eye fell on a little glass box lying under the table. She opened it and found in it a very small cake, on which the words "EAT ME" were beautifully marked in currants.

"Well, I'll eat it," said Alice, "and if it makes me grow larger, I can reach the key, and if it makes me grow smaller, I can creep under the door. Either way I'll get into the garden!"

Very soon she finished off the cake.

Chapter Two

The Pool of Tears

"Curiouser and curiouser!" cried Alice (she was so much surprised, that for the moment she quite forgot how to speak good English). "Now I'm opening out like the largest telescope that ever was! Goodbye, feet!"

Just at this moment her head struck against the roof of the hall: she was now rather more than nine feet high. She at once took up the little golden key and hurried off to the garden door.

Poor Alice! It was as much as she could do, lying down on one side, to look through the garden with one eye. To get through was more hopeless than ever. She sat

down and began to cry again.

She shed gallons of tears, until there was a pool all round her, about four inches deep and reaching halfway down the hall.

After a time she heard a little pattering of feet in the distance, and she hastily dried her eyes to see what was coming. It was the White Rabbit returning, splendidly dressed, with a pair of white kid gloves in one hand and a large fan in the other. He came trotting along in a hurry, muttering to himself, as he came, "Oh! the Duchess, the Duchess! Oh! *won't* she be savage if I've kept her waiting!"

Alice felt so desperate that she was ready to ask help of anyone: so, when the Rabbit came near her, she began, in a low, timid voice, "If you please, sir—"

The Rabbit started violently, dropped the white kid gloves and the fan, and scurried away into the darkness as hard as he could go.

Alice took up the fan and gloves, and, as the hall was very hot, she kept fanning herself all the time she went on talking.

"Dear, dear! How queer everything is today! And yesterday things went on just as usual. I wonder if I've been changed in the night?"

As she said this, she looked

down at her hands, and was surprised to see that she had put on one of the Rabbit's little white kid gloves while she was talking.

"How *can* I have done that?" she thought. "I must be growing small again." She found that she was now about two feet high, and was going on shrinking rapidly. She soon found out the cause of this was the fan she was holding, and she dropped it hastily, just in

time to save herself from shrinking away altogether.

"That *was* a narrow escape!"
said Alice, a good deal frightened.
"And now for the garden!" She
ran back to the little door; but,
alas! the little door was shut again,
and the little golden key was lying
on the glass table as before. "And
things are worse than ever," thought
the poor child, "for I never was so
small as this before, never!"

As she said these words her foot slipped, and in another moment, *splash!* she was up to her chin in salt water. Her first idea was that she had somehow fallen into the sea. However, she soon made out that she was in the pool of tears which she had wept when she was nine feet high.

"I wish I hadn't cried so much!" said Alice, as she swam about, trying to find her way out.

Just then she heard something splashing about in the pool a little way off. At first she thought it must be a walrus or hippopotamus, but then she remembered how small she was, and she soon made out that it was only a mouse.

"Would it be of any use, now," thought Alice, "to speak to the Mouse? At any rate, there's no harm in trying." So she began: "O Mouse, do you know the way out

of this pool? I am very tired of
swimming about here!"

The Mouse looked at her rather
inquisitively, and seemed to her to
wink with one of its little eyes.
"I'll be honored to escort you to
the shore," it seemed to say.

It was high time to go, for the
pool was getting quite crowded
with the birds and animals that had
fallen into it: there was a Duck
and a Dodo, a Lory and an Eaglet,

and several other curious creatures.
Alice led the way, and the whole
party swam to the shore.

Chapter Three

A Caucus Race

They were indeed a queer-look-
ing party that assembled on the
bank—the birds with draggled feath-
ers, the animals with their fur cling-
ing close to them, and all dripping
wet, cross, and uncomfortable.

At last the Dodo solemnly rose to its feet and said: "I suggest that the best thing to get us dry would be a Caucus race."

"What *is* a Caucus race?" said Alice; not that she much wanted to know, but the Dodo had paused as if it thought that somebody ought to speak, and no one else seemed inclined to say anything.

"Why," said the Dodo, "the best way to explain it is to do it." (And, as you might like to try the thing yourself, some winter day, I will tell you how the Dodo managed it.)

First it marked out a race course, in a sort of circle, and then all the party were placed along the course, here and there. There was no "One, two, three, and away!" but they began running when they liked, and left off when they liked, so that it was not easy to know when

the race was over. However, when they had been running half an hour or so, and were quite dry again, the Dodo suddenly called out, "The race is over!" and they all crowded around it, panting, and asking, "But who has won?"

"*Everybody* has won!" announced the Dodo. "And *all* must have prizes."

"But who is to give the prizes?" quite a chorus of voices asked.

"Why, *she* of course," said the
Dodo, pointing to Alice. The whole
party crowded around her, calling
out in a confused way, "Prizes!
Prizes!"

Alice had no idea what to do,
and in despair she put her hand in
her pocket and pulled out a box of
candies. She handed them round
as prizes. There was
exactly one apiece.

All the animals

39

cheered and then wandered off one by one, leaving Alice quite alone.

Poor Alice began to cry again, for she felt very lonely and low-spirited.

In a little while, however, she again heard a little pattering of footsteps in the distance, and she looked up eagerly to see who might be coming.

Chapter Four

The Rabbit Sends a Bill

It was the White Rabbit, trotting slowly back again, and looking anxiously about as it went, as if it had lost something. She heard it muttering to itself, "The Duchess! The Duchess! Oh my dear paws! Oh my fur and whiskers! Where *can* I have dropped them, I wonder?"

Very soon the Rabbit noticed Alice, and called out to her, in an angry tone, "Why, Mary Ann, what are you doing out here? Run home this moment, and fetch me a pair of gloves and a fan! Quick, now!" And Alice was so much frightened that she ran off at once in the direction it pointed to, without trying to explain the mistake that it had made.

"He took me for his house-maid," she said to herself as she ran. "How surprised he'll be when he finds out who I am! But I'd better take him his fan and gloves—that is, if I can find them."

As she said this, she came upon a neat little house, on the door of which was a bright brass plate with the name "W. RABBIT" engraved

upon it. She went in without knocking, and hurried upstairs, in great
fear lest she should meet the real
Mary Ann, and be turned out of
the house before she had found
the fan and gloves.

She found her way into a tidy
little room with a table in the window, and on it (as she had hoped)
a fan and two or three pairs of tiny
white kid gloves. She took up the
fan and a pair of the gloves, and

was just going to leave the room, when her eye fell upon a little bottle that stood near the looking-glass. There was no label this time with the words "DRINK ME," but nevertheless she uncorked the bottle and put it to her lips.

"I know *something* interesting is sure to happen," she said to herself.

Before she had drunk half the bottle, she found her head pressing against the ceiling, and had to stoop to save her neck from being broken.

She went on growing. As a last resource, she put one arm out of the window, and one foot up the chimney, and said to herself, "Now I can do no more, whatever happens. What *will* become of me?"

Luckily for Alice, the little magic bottle had now had its full effect, and she grew no larger. Still

it was very uncomfortable, and, as
there seemed to be no sort of chance
of her ever getting out of the room
again, no wonder she felt unhappy.

"Mary Ann! Mary Ann!" said
a voice outside. "Fetch me my gloves
this moment!" Presently the Rabbit came up to the door and tried
to open it; but, as the door opened
inwards, and Alice's elbow was
pressed hard against it, that at-
tempt proved a failure. Alice heard

it say to itself, "Then I'll go round and get in at the window."

"*That* you won't!" thought Alice, and, after waiting till she fancied she heard the Rabbit just under the window, she suddenly spread out her hand, and made a snatch in the air. She did not get hold of anything, but she heard a little shriek and a fall, and a crash of broken glass.

There was a long silence after

this, and Alice could only hear whispers now and then. She waited for some time without hearing anything more. At last came a rumbling of little cart wheels, and the sound of a good many voices all talking together. She made out the words: "*That* I won't, then! — Bill's got to go down — Here, Bill! The master says you've got to go down the chimney!"

"Oh! So Bill's got to come down

the chimney, has he?" said Alice
to herself. She drew her foot as far
down the chimney as she could,
and waited till she heard a little
animal (she couldn't guess what
sort it was) scratching and scram-
bling about in the chimney close
above her. Then she gave one sharp
kick, and waited to see what would
happen next.

The first thing she heard was
a general chorus of "There goes

Bill!" then the Rabbit's voice alone—"Catch him, you by the hedge!" then silence, and then another confusion of voices.

"I wonder what they'll do next," thought Alice to herself. The next moment a shower of little pebbles came rattling in at the window, and some of them hit her in the face.

Alice noticed, with some surprise, that the pebbles were all turning into little cakes as they lay on the floor, and a bright idea came into her head.

"If I eat one of these cakes," she thought, "it's sure to make some change in my size; and, as it can't possibly make me larger, it must make me smaller, I suppose."

So she swallowed one of the cakes, and was delighted to find that she began shrinking directly. As soon as she was small enough to get through the door, she ran out of the house, and found quite a crowd of little animals and birds waiting outside. They all made a rush at Alice the moment she appeared; but she ran off as hard as she could, and soon found herself safe in a thick wood.

"The first thing I've got to do," said Alice to herself, as she wandered about in the wood, "is to grow to my right size again; and the second thing is to find my way into that lovely garden. I think that will be the best plan. Let me see— how *am* I to grow up again? I suppose I ought to eat or drink something or other; but the great question is, 'What?' "

Alice looked all round her at

the flowers and the blades of grass, but she could not see anything that looked like the right thing to eat or drink. There was a large mushroom growing near her, about the same height as herself. When she had looked under it, and on both sides of it, and behind it, it occurred to her that she might as well look and see what was on top of it.

She stretched herself up on

tiptoe, and peeped over the edge of the mushroom. Her eyes immediately met those of a large blue caterpillar sitting on top, with its arms folded, quietly smoking a long hookah, and taking not the smallest notice of her or of anything else.

Chapter Five

Advice from a Caterpillar

The Caterpillar and Alice looked at each other for some time in silence. At last the Caterpillar took the hookah out of its mouth, and addressed her in a languid, sleepy voice.

"Who are *you*?" said the Caterpillar.

This was not an encouraging opening for a conversation. Alice replied, rather shyly, "I — I hardly know, sir, just at present — at least I know who I was when I got up this morning, but I think I must have been changed several times since then."

"What do you mean by that?" said the Caterpillar, sternly.

"Explain yourself!"

"I can't explain *myself*, I'm afraid, sir," said Alice, "because I'm not myself, you see."

"I don't see," said the Caterpillar.

"I'm afraid I can't put it more clearly," Alice replied very politely, "for I can't understand it myself, to begin with; and being so many different sizes in a day is very confusing."

"It isn't," said the Caterpillar.

Alice felt a little irritated at the Caterpillar's making such *very* short remarks, and seeing that the Caterpillar was in such an unpleasant state of mind, she turned away.

"Come back!" the Caterpillar called after her. "I've something important to say!"

This sounded promising, certainly. Alice turned and came back again.

For some minutes the Caterpillar puffed away without speaking. But at last it unfolded its arms, took the hookah out of its mouth again, and said, "So you think you're changed, do you?"

"I'm afraid I am, sir," said Alice. "I can't remember things as I used— and I don't keep the same size for ten minutes together!"

"Repeat *You Are Old, Father William*," said the Caterpillar.

Alice folded her hands and began:

"*You are old, Father William,*" *the young man said,*
"*And your hair has become very white;*
And yet you incessantly stand on your head —
Do you think, at your age, it is right?"

"In my youth," Father William
    replied to his son,
"I feared it might injure the brain;
But, now that I'm perfectly sure I
    have none,
Why, I do it again and again."

"You are old," said the youth, "as I
    mentioned before,
And have grown most uncommonly
    fat;

Yet you turned a back-somersault
   in at the door –
Pray what is the reason of that?"

"In my youth," said the sage, as he
   shook his grey locks,
"I kept all my limbs very supple
By the use of this ointment – one
   shilling the box –
Allow me to sell you a couple?"

"You are old," said the youth, "one
  would hardly suppose
That your eye was as steady as
  ever;
Yet you balanced an eel on the end
  of your nose –
What made you so awfully clever?"

"I have answered your questions,
  and that is enough,"
Said his father. "Don't give yourself airs!

*Do you think I can listen all day to
    such stuff?
Be off, or I'll kick you downstairs!"*

"It is wrong from beginning to
end," said the Caterpillar, decid-
edly. There was silence for some
minutes.

The Caterpillar then spoke.
"What size do you want to be?" it
asked.

"Well, I should like to be a

little larger, Sir, if you wouldn't mind," said Alice: "three inches is such a wretched height to be."

"It is a very good height indeed!" said the Caterpillar angrily, rearing itself upright as it spoke (it was exactly three inches high). It put the hookah into its mouth and began smoking again.

This time Alice waited patiently until it chose to speak again. In a minute or two the Caterpillar took

the hookah out of its mouth, and
yawned once or twice, and shook
itself. Then it got down off the
mushroom, and crawled away into
the grass, merely remarking, as it
went, "One side will make you
grow taller, and the other side will
make you grow shorter."

"One side of what? The other
side of what?" thought Alice to
herself.

"Of the mushroom," said the

Caterpillar, just as if she had asked it aloud. And in another moment it was out of sight.

Alice remained looking at the mushroom for a minute, trying to make out which were the two sides of it; and, as it was perfectly round, she found this very difficult. However, at last she stretched her arms round it as far as they would go, and broke off a bit of the edge with each hand.

"And now which is which?"

she said to herself, and
nibbled a little of the
right-hand bit to try the
effect. The next moment
she felt a violent blow underneath
her chin; it had struck her foot!

She set to work very carefully,
nibbling first at one bit and then
at the other, and growing
sometimes taller and
sometimes shorter, until

she had succeeded in
bringing herself to her
usual height.

"Come, there's half
my plan done now! I've
got back to my right size:
the next thing is, to get into that
beautiful garden. How *is* that to be
done, I wonder?" As she said this,
she came suddenly upon an open
place, with a little house in it about
four feet high.

"Whoever lives there," thought Alice, "it'll never do to come upon them this size: why, I should frighten them out of their wits!" So she began nibbling at the mushroom again, and did not venture near the house till she had brought herself down to nine inches high.

$\mathcal{P}$ig and Pepper

Alice went timidly up to the door, and knocked. There was a most extraordinary noise going on within — a constant howling and sneezing, and every now and then a great crash. Alice realized that nobody could possibly hear her knocking, so she opened the door and went in.

The door led right into a large kitchen, which was full of smoke from one end to the other. The Duchess was sitting on a three-legged stool in the middle, nursing a baby. The cook was leaning over the fire, stirring a large cauldron which seemed to be full of soup.

"There's certainly too much

pepper in that soup!" Alice said to herself, sneezing.

There was certainly too much of it in the *air*. Even the Duchess sneezed occasionally; and as for the baby, it was sneezing and howling alternately without a moment's pause. The only two creatures in the kitchen that did not sneeze were the cook and a large cat which was lying on the hearth and grinning from ear to ear.

"Please would you tell me," said Alice, a little timidly, for she was not quite sure whether it was good manners for her to speak first, "why your cat grins like that?"

"It's a Cheshire cat," said the Duchess, "and that's why. *Pig!*"

She said the last word with such sudden violence that Alice quite jumped; but she saw in another moment that it was addressed to the baby, and not to her, so she took courage, and went on again:

"I didn't know that cats *could* grin."

"You don't know much," said the Duchess; "and that's a fact."

Alice did not at all like the tone of this remark, and thought it would be as well to introduce some other subject of conversation. While she was

trying to fix on one, the cook took
the cauldron of soup off the fire,
and at once set to work throwing
everything within her reach at the
Duchess and the baby—the fire
irons came first; then followed a
shower of saucepans, plates, and
dishes. The Duchess took no notice of them, even when they hit
her; and the baby was howling so
much already, that it was quite
impossible to say whether the

blows hurt it or not.

"Oh, *please* mind what you're doing!" cried Alice, jumping up and down in terror.

"If everybody minded their own business," the Duchess said, in a hoarse growl, "the world would go round a deal faster. Here! You may nurse it a bit, if you like!" the Duchess said to Alice, flinging the baby at her as she spoke. "I must go play croquet with the Queen."

And she hurried out of the room. The cook threw a frying pan after her as she went, but it just missed her.

Alice caught the baby with some difficulty. She carried it out into the open air. "If I don't take this child away with me," thought Alice, "they're sure to kill it in a day or two. Wouldn't it be murder to leave it behind?" She said the last words out loud, and the little thing grunted in reply (it had left off sneezing by this time). "Don't grunt," said Alice; "that's not at all a proper way of expressing yourself."

The baby grunted again, and Alice looked very anxiously into its face to see what was the matter with it. There could be no mistake about it: it was neither more nor less than a pig. "If you're going to turn into a pig, my dear," said Alice, seriously, "I'll have nothing more to do with you."

She set the little creature down, and felt quite relieved to see it trot away quietly into the wood. "If it had grown up," she said to herself, "it would have made a dreadfully ugly child: but it makes rather a handsome pig, I think." And just then, she was a little startled by seeing the Cheshire Cat sitting on a bough of a tree a few yards off.

"Cheshire Puss," she began,

rather timidly, "what sort of people live about here?"

"In *that* direction," the Cat said, waving its right paw round, "lives a Hatter: and in *that* direction," waving the other paw, "lives a March Hare. Visit either you like: they're both mad." Then it began to fade away quite slowly, beginning with the end of the tail, and ending with the grin, which remained some time after the rest of it had gone.

Alice decided to visit the March Hare. She had not gone much farther before she came in sight of its house. She thought it must be the right house, because the chimneys were shaped like ears and the roof was thatched with fur. It was so large a house, that she did not like to go nearer till she had nibbled some more of the left-hand bit of mushroom, and raised herself to about two feet high. Even then she walked up towards it rather timidly, saying to herself, "Suppose it should be raving mad after all! I almost wish I'd gone to see the Hatter instead!"

Chapter Seven

A Mad Tea Party

There was a table set out under a tree in front of the house, and the March Hare and the Hatter were having tea at it. A Dormouse was sitting between them, fast asleep, and the other two were using it as a cushion, resting their elbows on it, and talking over its head. "Very uncomfortable for the Dormouse," thought Alice; "only, as it's asleep, I suppose it doesn't mind."

The table was a large one, but the three were all crowded together at one corner of it. Alice sat down in a large armchair at one end of the table.

"It wasn't very civil of you to

sit down without being invited," said the March Hare.

"I didn't know it was *your* table," said Alice: "it's laid for a great many more than three."

"Your hair wants cutting," said the Hatter. He had been looking at Alice for some time with great curiosity.

"You should learn not to make personal remarks," Alice said with some severity: "It's very rude."

The Hatter opened his eyes very wide on hearing this; but all he said was, "Why is a raven like a writing desk?"

"I believe I can guess that," said Alice.

"Do you mean that you think you can find out the answer to it?" said the March Hare.

"Exactly so," said Alice.

"Then you should say what you mean," the March Hare went on.

"I do," Alice hastily replied; "at least — at least I mean what I say — that's the same thing, you know."

"Not the same thing a bit!" said the Hatter. "Why, you might just as well say that 'I see what I eat' is the same thing as 'I eat what I see'! What day of the month is it?" he said. He had taken his watch

out of his pocket, and was looking at it uneasily, shaking it every
now and then, and holding it to
his ear.

Alice considered a lit-
tle, and then said, "The
fourth."

"Two days wrong!" sighed the
Hatter.

"What a funny watch!" Alice
remarked. "It tells the day of the

month, and doesn't tell what o'clock it is!"

"Have you guessed the riddle yet?" the Hatter said, turning to Alice.

"No, I give it up," Alice replied. "What's the answer?"

"I haven't the slightest idea," said the Hatter.

"Nor I," said the March Hare.

Alice sighed wearily. "I think you might do something better with the time," she said, "than wasting it in asking riddles that have no answers."

"If you know Time as well as I do," said the Hatter, "you wouldn't talk about wasting *it*. It's *him*."

"I don't know what you mean," said Alice.

The Hatter shook his head mournfully. "Time and I quarreled last March. It was at the great concert given by the Queen of

Hearts, and I had to sing:

> *Twinkle, twinkle, little bat!*
> *How I wonder what you're at!*
> *Up above the world you fly,*
> *Like a tea tray in the sky.*
> *Twinkle, twinkle —*

"Well, I'd hardly finished the first verse," said the Hatter, "when the Queen bawled out 'He's murdering the time! Off with his head!'"

"How dreadfully savage!" exclaimed Alice.

"And ever since that," the Hatter went on in a mournful tone, "it's always tea time, and we've no time to wash the things between whiles."

"Take some more tea," the March Hare said to Alice, very earnestly.

"I've had nothing yet," Alice

replied in an offended tone, "so I can't take more."

"You mean you can't take *less*," said the Hatter: "it's very easy to take *more* than nothing."

"Nobody asked your opinion," said Alice.

"Who's making personal remarks now?" the Hatter asked triumphantly.

Alice helped herself to some tea. "I don't think —"

"Then you shouldn't talk," said the Hatter.

This piece of rudeness was more than Alice could bear; she got up in great disgust, and walked off. No one took the least notice of her going, though she looked back once or twice, half hoping that they would call after her. The last time she saw them, they were trying to put the Dormouse into the teapot.

"At any rate, I'll never go there again!" said Alice, as she picked her way throught the wood. "It's the stupidest tea party I ever was at in all my life!"

Just as she said this, she noticed that one of the trees had a door leading right into it. "That's very curious!" she thought. "But everything's curious today. I think I may as well go in at once."

She set to work nibbling at the

mushroom (she had kept a piece of it in her pocket) till she was about a foot high. Then she walked through the little doorway. Then she found herself at last in the beautiful garden, among the bright flower beds and the cool fountains.

Chapter Eight

The Queen's Garden

A large rose tree stood near the entrance of the garden. The roses growing on it were white, but there were three gardeners at it, busily painting them red. Alice thought this a very curious thing, and she went nearer to watch them. She heard one of them say, "Look out now, Five! Don't go splashing paint over me like that!"

"I couldn't help it, Two," said Five, in a sulky tone. "Seven jogged my elbow."

Seven flung down his brush, and had just begun, "Well, of all the unjust things —" when his eye chanced to fall upon Alice, as she stood watching them, and he

checked himself suddenly. The others looked round also, and all of them bowed low.

"Would you tell me, please," said Alice, a little timidly, "why you are painting those roses?"

Two began, in a low voice, "Why, the fact is, you see, Miss, this here ought to have been a red rose tree, and we put a white one in by mistake; and, if the Queen was to find it out, we should all have our heads cut off. So you see, Miss, we're doing our best, afore she comes, to —"

At this moment, Five, who had been anxiously looking across the garden, called out "The Queen! The Queen!" and the three gardeners instantly threw themselves flat upon their faces. There was a sound of many footsteps, and Alice looked round, eager to see the Queen.

First came ten soldiers carrying clubs: these were all shaped like the three gardeners, oblong and flat, with their hands and feet at the corners. Next came ten courtiers: these were ornamented all over with diamonds. After these came the royal children: there were ten of them, and the little dears came jumping merrily along hand in hand, in couples; they were all ornamented with hearts. Next came the guests, mostly Kings and Queens, and among them Alice recognized the White Rabbit. It was talking in a hurried, nervous manner, smiling at everything that was said. Then followed the Knave of Hearts, carrying the King's crown on a velvet cushion; and, last of all in this grand procession, came

THE KING AND THE QUEEN OF HEARTS.

When the procession came opposite to Alice, they all stopped and looked at her, and the Queen said, "What's your name, child?"

"My name is Alice, so please your Majesty," said Alice very politely. But she added, to herself, "Why, they're only a pack of cards, after all. I needn't be afraid of them!"

"And who are *these*?" said the Queen, pointing to the three gardeners who were lying round the rose tree. "Get up!" she said in a shrill, loud voice. The three gardeners instantly jumped up, and began bowing to the King, the Queen, the royal children, and everybody else.

"May it please your Majesty," said Two, in a very humble tone, going down on one knee as he spoke, "we were trying —"

"I see!" said the Queen, who had meanwhile been examining the roses. "Off with their heads!" she yelled, and the procession moved on, three of the soldiers remaining behind to execute the unfortunate gardeners, who ran to Alice for protection.

"You shan't be beheaded!" said Alice, and she put them into a large flowerpot that stood near.

The three soldiers wandered about for a minute or two, looking for them, and then quietly marched off after the others. Alice followed.

"Are their heads off?" shouted the Queen.

"Their heads are gone, if it please your Majesty!" the soldiers shouted in reply.

"That's right!" shouted the Queen. "Can you play croquet?"

"Yes!" shouted Alice.

"Come on, then!" roared the Queen, and Alice joined the procession, wondering very much what would happen next.

"Get to your places!" shouted the Queen in a voice of thunder. People began running about in all directions, tumbling up against each other. However, they got settled down in a minute or two, and the game began.

Alice thought she had never

seen such a curious croquet ground
in her life. The croquet balls were
live hedgehogs, and the mallets
live flamingoes, and the soldiers
had to double themselves up and
stand on their hands and feet to
make the arches.

The chief difficulty Alice found
at first was in managing her flamingo. She succeeded in getting
its body tucked away comfortably
enough, under her arm, with its

legs hanging down, but generally,
just as she had got its neck nicely
straightened out, and was going to
give the hedgehog a blow, she would
find that the hedgehog had unrolled
itself and was in the act of crawl-
ing away.

The players all played at once,
without waiting for turns, quar-
relling all the while, and fighting
for the hedgehogs. In a very short
time the Queen was in a furious

passion, and went stamping about, shouting, "Off with his head!" or "Off with her head!" about once every minute.

Alice was wondering whether she could get away without being seen, when she noticed a curious appearance in the air. It puzzled her very much at first, but after watching it a minute or two she made it out to be a grin, and she said to herself, "It's the Cheshire

Cat: now I shall have somebody to talk to. But it's no use speaking to it till its ears have come."

In another minute the whole head appeared, and then Alice put down her flamingo, feeling very glad she had someone to listen to her. The Cat seemed to think that there was enough of it now in sight, and no more of it appeared.

"How do you like the Queen?"

said the Cat in a low voice.

"Not at all," said Alice, "she's so extremely—" Just then she noticed that the Queen was close behind her, listening, so she went on, "— likely to win, that it's hardly worthwhile finishing the game."

The Queen smiled.

"Who are you talking to?" said the King, coming up to Alice, and looking at the Cat's head with great curiosity.

"It's a friend of mine—a Cheshire Cat," said Alice.

"Was it invited?" asked the King very doubtfully.

"It belongs to the Duchess," said Alice, "you'd better ask her about it."

"She's in prison," the Queen said. She called to the executioner: "Fetch me the Duchess."

The Cat's head immediately began fading away, and by the time

the Duchess was brought, it had
entirely disappeared.

Chapter Nine

The Mock Turtle's Tale

"You can't think how glad I am to see you again, you dear old thing!" said the Duchess, as she tucked her arm affectionately into Alice's, and they walked off together.

Alice was very glad to find her in such a pleasant temper, and thought to herself that perhaps it was only the pepper that had made her so savage when they met in the kitchen.

"You're thinking about something, my dear," said the Duchess, "and that makes you forget to talk. I can't tell you just now what the moral of that is, but I shall remember it in a bit."

"Perhaps it hasn't one," Alice ventured to remark.

"Tut, tut, child!" said the Duchess. "Everything's got a moral, if only you can find it." And she squeezed herself up closer to Alice's side as she spoke.

"The game's going on rather better now," Alice said, by way of keeping up the conversation a little.

"'Tis so," said the Duchess, "and the moral of that is — 'Oh, 'tis love, 'tis love, that makes the world go round!'"

"Somebody said," Alice whispered, "that it's done by everybody minding their own business!"

"Ah, well! It means much the same thing," said the Duchess, digging her sharp little chin into Alice's shoulder as she added, "and the m——"

But here, to Alice's great surprise, the Duchess's voice died away, even in the middle of her favorite word 'moral,' and the arm that was linked into hers began to tremble. Alice looked up, and there stood the Queen in front of them, with her arms folded, frowning like a thunderstorm.

"A fine day, Majesty!" the Duchess began in a weak voice.

"Now, I give you fair warning," shouted the Queen, stamping on the ground as she spoke;

"either you or your head must be off, and that in about half no time! Take your choice!"

The Duchess took her choice, and was gone in a moment.

Then the Queen said to Alice: "Have you seen the Mock Turtle?"

"No," said Alice. "I don't even know what a Mock Turtle is."

"It's the thing Mock Turtle Soup is made from," said the Queen.

"I never saw one, or heard of one," said Alice.

"Come on, then," said the Queen, "and he shall tell you his history."

They very soon came upon a Gryphon, lying asleep in the sun. "Up, lazy thing!" said the Queen, "and take this young lady to see the Mock Turtle, and to hear his history. I must see after some executions I have ordered"; and

she walked off, leaving Alice alone
with the Gryphon. Alice did not
quite like the look of the creature,
but on the whole she thought it
would be quite as safe to stay with
it as to go after that savage Queen;
so she waited.

The Gryphon sat up and rubbed
its eyes. Then it watched the Queen
till she was out of sight. Then it
chuckled. "What fun!" said the
Gryphon, half to itself, half to Alice.

"What is the fun?" said Alice.

"Why, she," said the Gryphon. "It's all her fancy, that: they never executes nobody, you know. Come on!"

They had not gone far before they saw the Mock Turtle in the distance, sitting sad and lonely on a little ledge of rock. As they came nearer, Alice could hear him sighing as if his heart would break. She pitied him deeply.

"What is his sorrow?" she asked the Gryphon. And the Gryphon answered, very nearly in the same words as before, "It's all his fancy, that: he hasn't got no sorrow, you know. Come on!"

So they went up to the Mock Turtle, who looked at them with large eyes full of tears, but said nothing.

"This here young lady," said the Gryphon, "she wants to know your history."

"I'll tell it her," said the Mock Turtle, in a deep, hollow tone. "Sit down, both of you, and don't speak a word till I've finished."

So they sat down, and nobody spoke for some minutes. Alice thought to herself, "I don't see how he can ever finish, if he doesn't begin." But she waited patiently.

"Once," said the Mock Turtle at last, with a deep sigh, "I was a real Turtle. When we were little, we went to school in the sea. The master was an old Turtle — we used to call him Tortoise—"

Why did you call him Tortoise, if he wasn't one?" Alice asked.

"We called him Tortoise because he taught us," said the Mock Turtle angrily. "Really, you are very dull!"

"You ought to be ashamed of yourself for asking such a simple question," added the Gryphon. Then they both sat silent and looked at poor Alice, who felt ready to sink into the earth. At last the Gryphon said to the Mock Turtle, "Drive on, old fellow! Don't be all day about it!" and he went on in these words:

"Yes, we went to school in the sea. We had the best of educations. I took Reeling and Writhing, to begin with, and then the different branches of Arithmetic — Ambition, Distraction, Uglification and Derision."

"And how many hours a day did you do lessons?" asked Alice.

"Ten hours the first day," said the Mock Turtle: "nine the next, and so on."

"What a curious plan!" exclaimed Alice.

"That's the reason they're called lessons," the Gryphon remarked:

"because they lessen from day to day."

This was quite a new idea to Alice, and she thought it over a little before she made her next remark. "Then the eleventh day must have been a holiday?"

"Of course it was," said the Mock Turtle.

"That's enough about lessons," the Gryphon interrupted. "Tell her something about the games now."

Chapter Ten

The Lobster Quadrille

The Mock Turtle sighed, and drew the back of one flapper across his eyes. With tears running down his cheeks, he said:

"You may not have lived much under the sea —" ("I haven't," said

Alice) "—and perhaps you were never even introduced to a lobster —" (Alice began to say "I once tasted —" but checked herself hastily, and said, "No, never") "— so you can have no idea what a delightful thing a Lobster Quadrille is!"

"It must be a very pretty dance," said Alice timidly.

"Come, let's try the first figure!" said the Mock Turtle to the

Gryphon. "We can do it without lobsters, you know. Which shall sing?"

"Oh, you sing," said the Gryphon. "I've forgotten the words."

So they began solemnly dancing round and round Alice, every now and then treading on her toes when they passed too close, and waving their forepaws to mark the time, while the Mock Turtle sang

this, very slowly and sadly:

"Will you walk a little faster?"
  said a whiting to a snail,
"There's a porpoise close behind
  us, and he's treading on my
  tail.
See how eagerly the lobsters and
  the turtles all advance!
They are waiting on the shingle —
  will you come and join the
  dance?

*Will you, won't you, will you, won't
    you, will you join the dance?*

"*You can really have no notion
    how delightful it will be
When they take us up and throw
    us, with the lobsters, out to
    sea!*"
*But the snail replied "Too far, too
    far!" and gave a look askance,
Said he thanked the whiting kindly,
    but he would not join the dance.*

155

Would not, could not, would not,
    could not,
Would not join the dance.
Would not, could not, would not,
    could not,
Could not join the dance.

"What matters it how far we go?"
    his scaly friend replied.
"There is another shore, you know,
    upon the other side.
The further off from England the

nearer is to France —
Then not turn pale, beloved snail,
 but come and join the dance.
Will you, won't you, will you, won't
 you
Will you join the dance?"

"Thank you, it's a very interesting dance to watch," said Alice,
feeling very glad that it was over
at last, "and I do so like that curious song about the whiting! But,

if I'd been the whiting, I'd have said to the porpoise, 'Keep back, please! We don't want you with us!'"

"They were obliged to have him with them," the Mock Turtle said. "No wise fish would go anywhere without a porpoise."

"Wouldn't it, really?" said Alice, in a tone of great surprise.

"Of course not," said the Mock Turtle. "Why, if a fish came to *me*, and told me he was going a journey, I should say 'With what porpoise?'"

"Don't you mean 'purpose'?" said Alice.

"I mean what I say," the Mock Turtle replied in an offended tone.

"Shall we try another figure of the Lobster Quadrille?" asked the Gryphon. "Or would you like the Mock Turtle to sing you another song?"

"Oh, a song, please, if the Mock Turtle would be so kind," Alice replied, so eagerly that the Gryphon said, in a rather offended tone, "Hm! No accounting for tastes! Sing her *Turtle Soup*, will you, old fellow?"

The Mock Turtle sighed deeply, and began, in a voice choked with sobs, to sing this:

Beautiful Soup, so rich and green,
Waiting in a hot tureen!
Who for such dainties would not
    stoop?
Soup of the evening, beautiful Soup!
Soup of the evening, beautiful Soup!
Beau-ootiful Soo-oop!
Beau-ootiful Soo-oop!
Soo-oop of the e-e-evening,
Beautiful, beauti-FUL SOUP!

"Chorus again!" cried the Gryphon, and the Mock Turtle had just begun to repeat it, when a cry of "The trial's beginning!" was heard in the distance.

"Come on!" cried the Gryphon, and, taking Alice by the hand, it hurried off, without waiting for the end of the song.

"What trial is it?" Alice panted as she ran, but the Gryphon only answered "Come on!" and ran faster,

while more and more faintly came,
carried on the breeze that followed
them, the melancholy words:

Soo-oop of the e-e-evening,
Beautiful, beautiful Soup!

$\mathcal{W}$ho Stole the Tarts?

The King and Queen of Hearts were seated on their throne when they arrived, with a great crowd assembled about — all sorts of birds and beasts, as well as the whole pack of cards. The Knave was standing before them, in chains, with a soldier on each side to guard him. Near the King was the White Rabbit, with a trumpet in one hand, and a scroll of parchment in the other.

In the very middle of the court was a table, with a large dish of tarts upon it. They looked so good that it made Alice quite hungry to look at them — "I wish they'd get the trial done," she thought, "and

hand round the refreshments!"
But there seemed to be no chance
of this; so she began looking at
everything about her to pass the
time.

Alice had never been in a court
of justice before, but she had read
about them in books. "That's the
judge," she said to herself, "because of his great wig."

The judge, by the way, was the
King; and, as he wore his crown

over the wig, he did not look at all comfortable, and it was certainly not becoming.

"And that's the jury box," thought Alice; "and those twelve creatures," (she was obliged to say "creatures," you see, because some of them were animals), "I suppose they are the jurors."

"Silence in the court!" cried the White Rabbit, and the King put on his spectacles and looked anxiously round, to make out who was talking.

"Herald, read the accusation!" said the King.

On this the White Rabbit blew three blasts on the trumpet, and then unrolled the parchment scroll, and read as follows:

"The Queen of Hearts, she made some tarts,
All on a summer day:

The Knave of Hearts, he stole those tarts
And took them quite away!"

"Call the first witness," said the King; and the White Rabbit blew three blasts on the trumpet, and called out "First witness!"

The first witness was the Hatter. He came in with a teacup in one hand and a piece of bread and butter in the other. "I beg pardon,

your Majesty," he began, "for bringing these in; but I hadn't quite finished my tea when I was sent for."

Here the Queen put on her spectacles, and began staring hard at the Hatter, who turned pale and fidgeted.

"Give your evidence," said the King, "and don't be nervous, or I'll have you executed on the spot."

This did not seem to encourage

the witness at all. In his confusion
he bit a large piece out of his
teacup instead of the bread and
butter.

Just at this moment Alice felt
a very curious sensation, which
puzzled her a good deal until she
made out what it was. She was
beginning to grow larger again, and
she thought at first she would get
up and leave the court; but on
second thought she decided to

remain where she was as long as there was room for her.

"I wish you wouldn't squeeze so," said the Dormouse, who was sitting next to her. "I can hardly breathe." All this time the Queen had never left off staring at the Hatter. She said, to one of the officers of the court, "Bring me the list of the singers in the last concert!" on which the wretched

Hatter trembled so, that he shook off both his shoes.

"Give your evidence," the King repeated angrily, "or I'll have you executed, whether you are nervous or not."

The miserable Hatter dropped his teacup and bread and butter, and went down on one knee. "I'm a poor man, your Majesty," he began.

"You're a *very* poor *speaker*," said the King. "If that's all you know about it, you may stand down."

"I can't go no lower," said the Hatter: "I'm on the floor."

"You may go," said the King, and the Hatter hurriedly left the court, without even waiting to put his shoes on.

"Call the next witness!" said the King.

The next witness was the Duchess's cook. She carried the pepper box in her hand, and Alice guessed who it was, even before she got into the court, by the way the people near the door began sneezing all at once.

"Give your evidence," said the King.

"Shan't," said the cook.

After folding his arms and frowning at the cook till his eyes were nearly out of sight, the King said in a deep voice, "What are tarts made of?"

"Pepper, mostly," said the cook.

"Treacle," said a sleepy voice behind her.

"Collar that Dormouse!" the Queen shrieked. "Behead that Dormouse! Turn that Dormouse out of court! Suppress him! Pinch him! Off with his whiskers!"

For some minutes the whole

court was in confusion, getting the
Dormouse turned out, and, by the
time they had settled down again,
the cook had disappeared.

"Never mind!" said the King,
with an air of great relief. "Call
the next witness."

Alice watched the White
Rabbit as he fumbled over the
list, feeling very curious to see
what the next witness would be
like, "– for they haven't got much

evidence *yet*," she said to herself. Imagine her surprise, when the White Rabbit read out, at the top of his shrill little voice, the name "Alice!"

Chapter Twelve

Alice's Evidence

"Here!" cried Alice, quite forgetting in the flurry of the moment how large she had grown in the last few minutes. She jumped up in such a hurry that she tipped over the jury box with the edge of her skirt, upsetting all the jurymen on to the heads of the crowd below, and there they lay sprawling about, reminding her very much of a globe of goldfish she had accidentally upset the week before.

"Oh, I *beg* your pardon!" she exclaimed in a tone of great dismay, and began picking them up again as quickly as she could. "As soon as the jury had a little recovered from the shock of being upset, the King addressed Alice: "What do you know about this business?"

"Nothing," said Alice.

"Nothing *whatever?*" persisted the King.

"Nothing whatever," said Alice.

"That's very important," the King said, turning to the jury. The White Rabbit interrupted: "Un-important, your Majesty means of course," he said, in a very respect-ful tone, but frowning and making faces at him as he spoke.

"*Un*important, of course, I meant," the King hastily said. He busily wrote in his notebook for some time, and then called out, "Consider your verdict!"

"No, no!" said the Queen. "Sentence first — verdict afterwards."

"Stuff and nonsense!" said Alice loudly. "The idea of having the sentence first!"

"Hold your tongue!" said the

Queen, turning purple.

"I won't!" said Alice.

"Off with her head!" the Queen shouted at the top of her voice. Nobody moved.

"Who cares for *you*?" said Alice (she had grown to her full size by this time). "You're nothing but a pack of cards!"

At this the whole pack rose up into the air, and came flying down upon her; she gave a little scream,

half of fright and half of anger, and tried to beat them off, and found herself lying on the bank, with her head in the lap of her sister, who was gently brushing away some dead leaves that had fluttered down from the trees upon her face.

"Wake up, Alice dear!" said her sister. "Why, what a long sleep you've had!"

"Oh, I've had such a curious dream!" said Alice. And she told her sister, as well as she could remember them, all these strange Adventures of hers that you have just been reading about; and, when she had finished, her sister kissed her, and said, "It was a curious dream, dear, certainly; but now run in to your tea; it's getting late."

So Alice got up and ran off, thinking while she ran, as well she might, what a wonderful dream it had been.

This book has been bound
using handcraft methods, and
Smyth-sewn to ensure durability.

The dust jacket
was designed by
Toby Schmidt.

The cover and interior
illustrations are by
Graham Evernden.

The interior
was designed by
Robert Perry.

The text was set in
Bernhard Modern
by Richard Conklin.